THE MIRACLE OF THE
AUGUST SNOW

BY CLAUDIA CANGILLA MCADAM

Illustrated by Oliver Cuthbertson

Huntington, Indiana

Our Sunday Visitor Publishing Division
Our Sunday Visitor, Inc.
200 Noll Plaza
Huntington, IN 46750
www.osv.com
1-800-348-2440

ISBN: 978-1-68192-798-5 (Inventory No. T2815)
1. JUVENILE FICTION—Religious—Christian—Historical.
2. JUVENILE FICTION—Religious—Christian—People & Places.
3. RELIGION—Christianity—Catholic.

LCCN: 2024931712

Cover and interior design: Lindsey Riesen
Cover and interior art: Oliver Cuthbertson

PRINTED IN THE UNITED STATES OF AMERICA

DEDICATION

With love for the beautiful and faith-filled
women who married my sons —
Sarah Norcross McAdam and Christine Wright McAdam,
the daughters of my heart.
— C.C.M.

ANCIENT ROME

CIRCUS MAXIMUS

EMPEROR'S PALACE

TO THE TIBER RIVER

THE VILLA

AQUEDUCT

1

THE CHASE

The twins raced through the front door of the villa, a large house in Rome. It was the home of a wealthy man and his wife. The boys' mama and papa worked for the owners, Master Giovanni and Mistress Julia.

The twins' bare feet slapped against the stone floor. Paulus ran behind Ignatius, holding a fishing pole like a sword. He poked his brother in the back with it. Then he did it again.

"Leave me alone!" Ignatius shouted. He clenched a

bundle of twine close to his chest.

"Then give that back!" Paulus demanded.

The boys tore through the entry hall. They dashed into the atrium, the main part of the house. They circled the shallow pool in the center of the room. Light poured through the large opening in the roof. Rainwater could fall into the pool. If only it would rain!

The twins zoomed past their mother, who was polishing a brass lamp.

"Halt!" their mother commanded.

Paulus chased Ignatius around a column. A delicate vase on top of a stand wobbled. The boys slid to a stop.

"Mama, make him —," the boys begged at the same time, pointing at each other.

"Quiet," their mother whispered as she steadied the vase. Her eyes darted to the chapel down the hallway leading out of the atrium.

The boys looked at each other and then at their mother.

"Is it Master Giovanni and his wife?" Ignatius asked.

"Are they in there praying again?" his brother

questioned.

"Yes," she answered, "and I want you to be quiet."

"But they are always in there," Ignatius said.

His mother pressed her finger against her lips. "Shush!"

In a softer voice, Paulus asked, "Why do they spend so much time in the chapel?"

Mama's eyebrows lifted, and she dipped her head toward her sons. "You two could take a lesson. Perhaps more time in prayer would give you less time for arguing."

She took the fishing pole from Paulus, and she held out her hand for Ignatius to give her the bundle of twine. "When the master and mistress are finished in the chapel, I think a few minutes on your knees in there might be a good idea." Their mother's eyes narrowed in a way that let the boys know she wasn't just making a suggestion.

"Now, go spend some time in the chapel," she said. "Then go outside and finish your chores."

"But it stinks out there," Paulus complained. "I think Antonia's father let some meat rot in the sun. Again." The father of their friend Antonia owned the market. But his memory wasn't that good. Once before, he had left a delivery of meat out in the alley.

"Yes, it's so hot outside," Ignatius grumbled. He eyed the water in the pool with longing.

His brother swiped at the sweat on his forehead. "Papa says he doesn't need fire to forge iron today, just the sun."

"I know," Mama said as she dabbed at the back of her neck with the polishing cloth. "It is the warmest month of Augustus we have ever had." She flapped her apron to fan her face.

It hadn't occurred to the boys that Mama might be uncomfortable in the heat, too. Cleaning was bad enough. But she also had food to prepare. Stirring boiling pots at mealtime must make her feel like she was cooking herself.

She smiled at the boys. "But we all have to work." She gestured to a large copper basin resting just inside the doorway. They had never seen it before. It looked like something to wash clothes in. Or for taking a bath. Whose was it?

2

Whispered Words

"Papa hammered out the dent in that tub," Mama said. "And it was hard work. Marco and Crispin will be coming soon to take it back home."

Marco and Crispin. They were brothers, and their father owned the villa down the lane. They must have brought the dented basin to Papa to repair. The twins were sure one of those boys must have damaged it.

Mama hugged them. "When you are done with your work," she said, "you may go fishing."

The boys' faces brightened. "That is," Mama stated in her most strict voice, "as long as there is no more arguing."

The boys' heads nodded more rapidly than a woodpecker's beak at work. Mama handed the fishing pole to Ignatius. She tossed the ball of twine to Paulus, then she shooed the twins away.

"And remember where you need to stop before you go outside to finish your chores."

"Yes, Mama," they said.

"Now, no noise on your way out!"

The twins tiptoed from the atrium and down the hallway. The door to the chapel stood open, and they peeked in.

Master Giovanni and his wife, Julia, knelt side by side. The couple leaned toward each other. Their heads nearly touched. Their hushed voices hummed like bees in a hive.

"Lord," Giovanni prayed, his eyes fixed on the crucifix above the altar. "We beg your help." He glanced at his wife and then returned his gaze to the cross. "You have greatly blessed us, and we thank you. But something is heavy on our hearts. When we die, we have no children to inherit our estate."

In the hall outside the chapel door, Paulus looked to Ignatius. The corners of his mouth twitched up. "They could leave all their money to us," he whispered.

Mistress Julia added her plea. "We will provide well for those who work for us," she said. Ignatius stood up tall and shot his brother a stern look.

"But with the rest of our wealth," Julia continued, "we want to honor your mother, Lord Jesus."

"Blessed Virgin Mary, please show us how we can do that," Giovanni said.

"Amen," they prayed together, their voices as soft as a purring kitten. They rose from their knees, straightened their garments, and turned to exit the chapel.

The boys ducked around a corner. When the master and his wife were out of sight, Paulus started to walk away from the chapel. Ignatius snagged the back of his tunic.

"Remember, we promised Mama that we would pray," he said as he tugged his brother into the chapel.

They knelt and clasped their hands. Just then from somewhere in the villa, a big crash boomed. The bang echoed through the halls. The boys looked at each other, their eyes as round as dinner plates.

3

CHORES

"**I** wonder what that noise was?" Paulus asked.

Ignatius glanced back over his shoulder. "I don't know. I'm just glad it wasn't because of *us*!"

"This time," Paulus said.

They bowed their heads, and each boy muttered a quick prayer of thanks that neither of them had caused the crash.

In the courtyard, the sun sizzled the backs of the boys' necks.

Through the open door to the workshop, they could see Papa. He used tongs to remove a length of metal from the fire. Its tip glowed bright red. "I'm fixing the harness for the horse," he told them.

Sweat streamed down his face as he hammered the metal. While it was still glowing, Papa used the tongs to help shape it into a hook. Then he plunged it into a bucket of water. Steam rose with a hiss.

"Let's work where it's cool," Ignatius suggested to Paulus. They settled outdoors on the shady side of the workshop.

Ignatius grabbed an armful of long slender branches. He picked one up and trimmed the wood. He stripped it of leaves and smoothed the surface. It would make an excellent fishing pole. He reached for the next branch.

Paulus sat nearby, twisting handfuls of dried grass into thick rope. In silence, the boys worked for an hour.

"Finally," Paulus said, gathering a big coil of rope into

his arms. "I've been working on this for a week. Now it's long enough for the water bucket to reach the bottom of the new well." He spread animal fat on the rope to waterproof it, then he stretched it on the ground to dry in the sun.

"Are you done?" he asked his brother.

"Almost," Ignatius answered.

Paulus ducked into the workshop. He scooted out with a bit of charcoal. He also carried a piece of wood. Ignatius recognized it as having been a side panel on a wrecked cart.

"What are you doing?" Ignatius asked.

Paulus sketched on the wood. "One day when we open our shop for selling our fishing poles, we'll need a sign. I'm drawing one."

Ignatius smiled. "I've already built a small version of what the shop will look like." He reached under the bench set against the corner of the shop. He lifted up a small wooden building. It had two window openings. There was even a little door that swung open.

Paulus nodded his support. "All that's missing is us!"

Ignatius put the model back under the bench. He finished sanding the last pole. He stood it with the others against the side of the workshop. "I'm done with my work. Where's the fishing line you made?" he asked.

Paulus set his sketch down on the ground. He fetched a mass of thin twine he had woven, already coated with fat and dried. He cut off a length for himself and one for Ignatius.

Each boy selected a pole, tied one end of twine to it, and looped the other end through a hook made of bone.

"These are the best fishing poles in all of Rome," Ignatius declared. "Before we sell any, I want to give the finest one to Pope Liberius the next time we see him. But first . . ." He grinned at his brother.

"Fishing!" they shouted together.

4

TO THE TIBER

"**B**ut what if the fish aren't biting?" Paulus asked.

Ignatius patted his waist. He had tied a small cloth bag onto his belt. "I'm bringing the marbles," he said with a grin. "We'll have fun no matter what we do."

The boys slipped out through the gate of the villa carrying their fishing poles. The strong smell of rotten meat hooked their nostrils. They breathed in through their mouths.

Master Giovanni and his wife were climbing into a

carriage. Their father attached the repaired harness to the horse.

"Going fishing?" Master Giovanni called out to them. The boys nodded and raised their poles.

Mistress Julia waved to them. "Bring back something tasty for dinner," she called. "We're off to see Pope Liberius!"

———◦————————◦———

Paulus waved back as Ignatius stared off into the distance. His eyes followed the aqueduct, the waterway bringing fresh water into Rome. Three towering rows of red stone arches, one on top of the other, stretched like an arm reaching into Rome.

Paulus turned to look at the aqueduct with his brother. The red color made him smile. It reminded him of a vein bringing life into the city. But it brought water, not blood.

"Someday, I want to build something as beautiful as that," Ignatius said.

A laugh broke out from behind him. Marco and his younger brother, Crispin,s stepped out from behind a tree.

"You, a builder, Ignatius?" Marco chuckled.

"What do *you* know about building anything?" Crispin asked, raking his hand through his curly hair.

Ignatius threw his shoulders back and took a swift step toward the boys. Paulus held him back with a hand on his brother's chest. "Don't let them bother you," he said.

"You're right," Ignatius agreed. "All these two are doing is keeping us from fishing."

The twins turned away and hurried along the stone lane. Marco and Crispin followed them. Soon they reached the Circus Maximus, the stadium for chariot races. Shouts and cheers roared from the stands. The sound of galloping hooves thundered on the air toward them.

Paulus stopped. His mouth hung open. The early afternoon sun shone on the stadium and the huge emperor's palace that rose next to it. The light bathed the stone of the buildings in a shade as rich as honey. "I love that color!" Paulus whispered.

"And the design," Ignatius said. "That's what I want to do."

"What?" asked Paulus. "Build another stadium? Or a new palace?"

Ignatius shook his head. "I don't know exactly what. Just something important."

"And I'd like to create the prettiest art for it," his brother said.

A pebble struck Ignatius in the back of his calf. Then one hit Paulus. They spun around to see Marco kicking little stones at them.

"You know," Marco said with a sneer, "you two could work in the Circus Maximus right now."

"Driving chariots?" his brother Crispin asked.

Marco snorted. "Oh, no. I meant they could rake the ground between the races. Or clean up the horses' dung." Both boys burst into loud laughter.

"You wouldn't need these any longer," Marco added as he tried to snatch Ignatius's fishing pole.

Ignatius yanked it away.

"Ouch!" Marco shouted. "Something poked me!"

"Serves you right," Ignatius said. "You grabbed the hook. Don't you know anything about fishing?"

The tips of Marco's ears turned red. "Crispin and I have more important things to do than to get wet and muddy in the Tiber River like slimy eels." He clutched his injured hand with the other and jerked his head to his

brother as a signal to leave.

"Why are they always so mean?" Paulus asked as he watched the boys go.

Ignatius shrugged and rested his fishing pole on his shoulder. "Maybe they wish they were as good at fishing as we are." He thought for a moment. "I wonder if they know how to fish at all."

"Well, *we* know how," said Paulus. He elbowed his brother. "I'll race you." With that, they flew to their favorite fishing spot.

They kicked off their sandals on the bank of the Tiber. The cool water licked their ankles. They spent the rest of the afternoon casting their lines into the dark water. They couldn't see the two boys hiding in the trees, watching them with envy.

5

THE VISIT

In the palace where he lived, Pope Liberius welcomed his friends.

"Giovanni and Julia, please, come in," he said. The couple bowed before the pope and kissed his ring.

The pope sat, and his visitors settled onto chairs. A servant placed refreshments before them. Giovanni and his wife told the pope the reason for their visit. Their wish was to leave their money to a worthy cause that would help the Faith. "We want to help people grow in their love

for Jesus and his mother," they said.

Pope Liberius listened carefully. He nodded when they explained that they had been praying to Mary for an answer. "You are most kind to pledge your wealth to the Church," he told them. "I, too, will ask our Heavenly Mother for her guidance in this matter."

He walked his friends to the door. They thanked him for his time.

"May God bless you for your generosity," the pope said as he made the sign of the cross over them.

"And may our prayers be answered," Giovanni said, not realizing how quickly that would happen.

<hr />

On the way home from the river, Paulus carried the two fishing poles. Ignatius slung a stringer of fish over his shoulder. The fishing had been excellent! Eight fish dangled from the line he carried. Their scales glittered like silver coins dancing in the sun.

They came near their neighbors' courtyard. The excited voices of kids floated over the trees. They recognized the voice of their friend Antonia.

"I won! I won!" she shouted.

The twins stopped at the gate to the courtyard. Marbles were scattered across the dirt. Marco and Crispin sat on the ground. Antonia stood next to them. As the winner of the game, her prize would be a marble from the loser. She bent down and plucked up a glass ball. She held it up to the sunlight.

"Blue, my favorite color," she said. "Thank you for the game, Marco. This is the third time in a row I've beaten you."

"It's too bad you don't have your father's memory," Marco grumbled. He pinched his nostrils together. Crispin laughed.

Marco gathered up his marbles and curled his upper lip at Antonia. Then he noticed the twins standing at the gate.

"How about you, Ignatius?" Marco jumped up. "Want to shoot some marbles?"

Ignatius spotted the fine leather bag hanging from Marco's belt. His own hand reached to his waist. His marbles crowded together inside the old cloth sack tied with a dirty piece of string.

The last time they had played, Ignatius had won Marco's very best marble. The color of amber, it looked like the eye of a cat. Did he want to risk losing it back to him?

6

THE GAME

"Come on," Marco said to Ignatius. "I'm not having a good day. I just lost to Antonia."

Ignatius considered the offer. If he won another contest with Marco, he could choose which of Marco's beautiful marbles he would like. But what if he lost?

Marco stared at him. He was daring Ignatius to play. Ignatius pushed the stringer of fish into Paulus's arms.

The boys dumped out their bags of marbles. A circle had been drawn in the dirt. The boys counted out an equal number of marbles. They would take turns shooting their marbles from behind a line drawn farther out. Whoever ended up with the most marbles in the circle would win.

The first two games, Ignatius and Marco got an equal number of marbles in the circle. On the third game, Ignatius had eight of his marbles stay in the circle. Marco only had seven inside. But he had one last marble to shoot.

Ignatius held his breath. If Marco missed, Ignatius would win. But if Marco's marble stayed in the circle, they would be tied again.

Marco knelt on one knee. He flicked his marble. Ignatius watched in horror as it knocked out one of his own marbles. Marco's marble stopped well inside the circle. Marco had won!

Ignatius held out the cat's eye marble to Marco. But Marco shook his head. "I want something else," he said.

Ignatius would be happy if Marco chose any of his other marbles.

Marco pointed to the stringer of fish Paulus had set

down.

"I want those," he said.

"No," cried Paulus. "You can't. That's our dinner!"

Marco considered. "Half of the fish, then."

Ignatius shook his head. "No. That won't leave us enough."

"Hmm," Marco hummed. "Two, then."

Ignatius nodded, but Marco wasn't finished. "And your second-best marble."

Ignatius handed over the only other glass marble he had. All the rest of his were made of hardened clay.

Marco's lips curved up in a wicked grin. He dropped the marble into his leather bag and lifted the two largest fish off the line.

Ignatius's chin sank to his chest. He swung the remaining fish over his shoulder. With Paulus trailing him, he stomped from the courtyard and headed home.

7

Home Again

"How was fishing?" their mother asked.

The boys handed Mama the line with six fish on it.

"What a splendid catch!" she exclaimed.

Ignatius whispered to Paulus from behind his hand. "Not as splendid as it would have been if Marco hadn't taken the two biggest ones."

"I will grill them outside for the master's dinner and ours," Mama said. "Thank you for keeping me from that boiling kitchen."

"Maybe the heat is why Marco and Crispin are being so mean," Ignatius said.

Paulus frowned. "No, they are *always* mean."

Their mother raised her eyebrows. "What happened?"

"They keep picking on us," Ignatius told her.

"They make fun of us and the things we want to do," Paulus added.

The boys said nothing about the game of marbles and the loss of the two fish.

Their mother tapped her chin. "Hmmm. Maybe they are jealous of you."

"Of *us*?" the boys asked together.

"Their parents own that big villa. They have everything they want," Ignatius said.

"Everything?" their mother asked. "You must have something they don't have. Are they happy?"

The boys dropped their heads.

"They weren't very happy when they came this morning to pick up the copper tub," she said.

The twins noticed the basin near the door. The *dented* basin.

"I thought Papa fixed it," Ignatius said.

Mama placed her hands on her hips. "He did. When Marco and Crispin came to pick it up, they argued about who would carry it home. They dropped it. Again. Papa will have to hammer out the new dent."

Paulus and Ignatius glanced at each other. They pressed their lips together to keep from laughing. So *that* was what had caused the noise when they were in the chapel.

Mama shooed them outside. "Now, put your fishing things away. Wash up and then bring the table to the porch. And draw me some water, please."

———

Inside Papa's workshop, the twins stored their fishing poles in a corner. They dipped their hands into a bucket of water and dried them on a rag. Through the open window, they could hear someone speaking with Papa outside.

"I'm sorry that you'll have to repair it once more," a man said. "Of course, I'll pay for your work again."

"Thank you, Master Maximus," Papa said. The boys looked at each other. It was the father of Marco and Crispin.

"My boys may be clumsy, but they seem to be excellent fishermen," he said. "I didn't even know they could fish. But you should see the two beauties they caught this afternoon!"

Ignatius started to say something, but Paulus placed his hand over his brother's mouth. "You don't want to call them liars to their father's face," he whispered. "He won't believe us, and it might cost Papa work."

Ignatius flung the rag to the floor and listened as Master Maximus walked away.

"Let's just get our tasks done," Paulus pleaded.

⚬───────────⚬

Ignatius tied an end of the new rope to the handle of the

bucket. He took it to the deep well and lowered it. But the other end of the rope slipped from his hand. The bucket dove down to the bottom of the shaft. The rope snaked after it.

"Oh, no!" he yelled, his voice echoing in the inky hole.

8

Gone

Paulus rushed from the other side of the courtyard where he was pulling benches up to the table. Fury blazed in his eyes. "What have you done? My best rope! That took me days to make!"

He threw his shoulder into his brother's waist. Ignatius crashed to the ground. Like a tumbleweed caught in a gust of wind, the twins rolled in the dirt. Puffs of dust rose around them like incense.

The fight caused them to barrel into the fishing poles

stacked against the side of the workshop. The wooden rods bent and snapped, splintering into sticks.

Ignatius's face turned pale. His eyes waterfalled with tears. "Look what you've done to my fishing poles!" he shouted. He stepped backward right onto the piece of wood with Paulus's charcoal drawing. He spun on his heel and stomped up the stone steps to the boys' room above the workshop.

Paulus brushed his fingers along the blurred edges of his artwork. He set it down and leaned into the blackness of the well. His knuckles grew white as he grasped the stone edge. Not only was his drawing damaged, but the bucket . . . and his rope . . . were gone.

All during dinner, the twins shot angry looks back and forth. After the meal, Ignatius stacked the splintered sticks that had once been his prized fishing poles. Paulus dabbed at his artwork with a damp cloth. Silence wrapped them both.

When their mother called them together for their nightly lesson from Holy Scripture, neither boy wanted to be there. They sat across the table from Mama, as far away from each other as possible.

Master Giovanni had a large library of scrolls, parchments, and books. He allowed Mama and Papa to use them to teach the twins. Tonight, Mama read from Paul's letter to the Romans. "Listen to what he wrote three hundred years ago," she said.

"We know that in everything God works for good with those who love him," Mama read, "who are called according to his purpose."

"In everything?" Ignatius asked.

"Yes," she said. "God doesn't cause bad things to happen to people. But he can bring good from it."

Paulus grunted. "Like how?"

"Well," she said. "Remember when Felix the baker dropped that large stone on his foot?"

"Yes," the twins said together.

"That certainly wasn't a good thing, was it?" The boys shook their heads.

Their mother continued. "He was supposed to leave the next day for a long journey. He couldn't go. The day after that, what happened?"

The boys remembered that Felix's son came home from the army. It was the first time they had seen each other in years.

"So, there is the good that God brought about," Mama said. "If Felix hadn't broken his foot, he would have been gone when his son returned."

"And when the fire destroyed Octavia's home?" Mama asked.

"Her friends built her another one," Ignatius said.

"Better than the first," Paulus added.

"Yes," Mama said. "Often God uses us to do his work." She moved her finger farther down in Paul's letter.

"He reminds us of Jesus' words," she said. "You shall love your neighbor as yourself."

She put the letter aside. "And who is even closer to you than your neighbor?" She looked from one of her sons to the other. Neither boy said a word.

Their mother sighed. "Now, off to bed, you two."

Squeezed into their narrow cot that night, their mother's words filled their heads. But still, they slept with their backs to each other.

9

The Dream

The next morning dawned as hot and sticky as the day before. The excited voices of Giovanni and Julia hacked through the heat. Their words tugged on the boys' ears, waking them slowly.

Ignatius and Paulus sat up. They refused to look at each other as they peered out the window.

The master and his wife stood in the courtyard below. They were speaking with Mama and Papa.

"Last night," Master Giovanni said, "we prayed to our

Blessed Mother. We asked how we could best honor her."

"And she answered us!" Julia added. She clutched Mama's arms. "The Virgin Mary appeared to us both in a dream. The same dream!"

Giovanni held his hands to his heart. "She asked us to build a church dedicated to her."

His wife's voice bubbled like water boiling in a pot. She could hardly hold back her excitement. "The Blessed Mother said we would know the place, because this morning, there would be snow lying on the site!" she exclaimed. "Imagine! Snow in summer!"

Snow!? It had only snowed in Rome once in the last decade. And that was in winter!

Ignatius and Paulus glanced briefly at each other and shoved away from the window. They sprinted down the stone steps together and bolted from the villa.

"How will we find the place?" Ignatius asked.

Keeping pace with his brother, Paulus answered. "A hill. We'll climb a hill to see."

They charged past the home of Marco and Crispin,

who ran out and followed them. "Where are you going?" they shouted.

The twins ignored them. They dashed through sizzling streets. They pushed past gorgeous gardens.

Under an arch of the aqueduct, they ran. They zipped past the oval arena where even now, they heard people cheering for battling gladiators.

Soon they reached the hills of Rome, Marco and Crispin on their heels.

"What's the hurry?" Marco yelled at them. "What is so important?"

"It . . . snowed . . . last . . . night," Ignatius answered.

"The Blessed Mother . . . said it would," Paulus panted. "We need . . . to find . . . where."

Marco and Crispin hooted. "Snow?" chuckled Marco. "Ha! This heat has fried your brains!"

Ignatius and Paulus didn't care if the brothers believed. They pumped their legs even harder.

Mama and Papa tried to keep up with the boys. Giovanni and Julia rushed after them. Soon, they were all out of breath. The boys were just dots in the distance. The adults stopped, exhausted. The burning sun stared down on them.

A familiar figure hurried up to the group.

"Your Holiness!" Giovanni cried, bending to kiss the pope's ring.

"Giovanni! Friends!" Pope Liberius said as he tried to catch his breath. "The most amazing thing has happened. Our Lady appeared to me in a dream last night. She asked that a church be built on land that would be marked by —, by —"

"Snow?" the others chimed in. The pope nodded, amazed.

Giovanni told the pope how he and his wife had the very same vision. Everyone stood in the scorching heat. The sun blistered their faces as they tried to make sense of the dream.

Far up ahead, the boys climbed a hill. It was level at the top. Ignatius and Paulus stopped quickly. Marco and Crispin crashed into them. The four boys stood frozen, gaping at the ground. How was it possible? How could it snow on the hottest night in August?

10

Snow

Marco and Crispin sank to the ground. Their mouths hung open wide. They couldn't make sense of what they saw.

The twins stared. Their eyes burned with tears of joy. And from the brightness of the snow that covered the field.

Racing back into the city, Ignatius and Paulus tore through the streets, elbowing each other out of the way. At last, they spied the cluster of people discussing the

shared dream.

"Holy Father!" Ignatius yelled, pushing past his brother.

"Master Giovanni!" Paulus shouted even louder.

They skidded to a stop. Each did his best to bow and show respect.

"Snow!" they gasped together. "On the Esquiline Hill!"

Everyone sped to the spot where a blanket of white stretched across the hilltop. It roughly sketched the shape of a church.

The pope fell to his knees. Giovanni and his wife knelt and pressed their foreheads to the ground.

"It's a miracle! A miracle!" exclaimed one person after another.

"We must mark the outline," the pope instructed, "before the snow melts!"

Ignatius and Paulus eyed each other. One thought bounced between them.

They hurried home and returned with a hammer, a bundle of twine, and arms full of sticks that were all that was left of the fishing poles they broke.

Quickly, they skirted the outline of the snow. They marked the shape with twine coiled around sticks driven into the ground. As they tightened the last knot, the sun licked up the snow. The twins grinned and hugged.

"I'm sorry about yesterday," Paulus said.

"Me, too," said Ignatius. "I never meant to lose your rope. Or to ruin your drawing."

"I know. And I'm sorry about your fishing poles."

They looked at the work they had completed. What had happened yesterday didn't seem to matter now.

Their parents stood behind them. They rested their hands on their sons.

Papa squeezed their shoulders. "Paul had it right," he said.

Mama leaned between them and whispered. "Remember what he said in his letter we read last night? He said, 'In all things, God works for good.' All things, boys."

"Never forget that," Papa added.

Ignatius and Paulus looked at the sticks that had once been fishing poles. Their eyes traced the line formed by every inch of their twine. They understood.

11

Building Plans

During the next few days, the boys went to the banks of the Tiber River. Ignatius cut more long, slender branches. Paulus gathered handfuls of long grass to twist into new twine. He searched the riverbed for small stones in shades of white, black, and brown.

In the evenings, Ignatius designed plans for a church. Master Giovanni gave him a sheet of paper made from the papyrus plant. Ignatius drew straight lines and rounded pillars. He arched an entry that reminded him of the aqueduct. He outlined a tall steeple.

Paulus washed and sorted his pebbles. He made a mosaic of the Blessed Mother on the backside of the old plank of wood. For glue, he used tar he made by burning birch bark.

When they were finished, they laid their creations on the table.

Papa tapped a finger on the sketch of the church. "That tower will need a bell," he said.

"I wonder if there is anyone who might be able to make one," Mama said, her eyes twinkling.

Papa scratched his chin as if thinking. "I believe I know someone who could forge a bell."

The twins laughed as they hugged Papa. He roughed up their hair. "It will take a good amount of copper, though. Now, you two, finish your chores and get cleaned up. An important visitor is coming to the villa this afternoon."

Later in the day, the pope visited to meet with Master

Giovanni. He wanted to plan the building of the church. He noticed Ignatius's sketch and Paulus's mosaic on the table. "I'd like to see the boys," he said to Master Giovanni.

Pope Liberius called Ignatius and Paulus to his side. He praised their quick thinking and ability to work together. "You knew just what to do when you saw the snow," he said. "I give you my thanks and a special blessing." The twins bowed their heads.

"It will take much work to construct this church for Mary," he told them.

Master Giovanni agreed. "The builders will need a lot of helpers," he said. "And apprentices to work with them."

He looked at the twins. "Do you know what an apprentice is?" They shook their heads "no."

"An apprentice is a student. It's a young person who learns a trade from someone who is very good at doing something."

The pope glanced at the twins' work on the table. "I wonder if there are any boys who would like to become builders?"

"Or artists of religious works such as paintings, statues, and mosaics," Master Giovanni added.

Ignatius and Paulus elbowed each other. Their hearts thumped wildly in their chests.

"It will take a long time to build this church," the pope explained. "The youngsters who help out in the beginning will be the ones to finish the job."

Julia walked up to the boys. "You, Paulus and Ignatius, will learn from those who already know how, and then you will pass the knowledge on to others. It is always important to teach others who want to learn a new skill," she added.

"Like fishing," Ignatius said.

Paulus exchanged a glance with his brother.

They ran to the new stack of fishing poles and selected four of them. They picked up some twine for fishing line and some hooks. They returned to the adults.

"We'll be back in a little while," Ignatius said.

Paulus grinned at them. "We're going to give some fishing lessons!"

12

GIFTS

The pope was still inside speaking with Master Giovanni when the boys returned.

In the courtyard, they saw Antonia handing Mama a wrapped bundle.

"My father sent a leg of lamb for you to prepare for the pope's dinner," she said.

The boys exchanged horrified glances.

"Don't worry," Antonia whispered. "I was at the market when the delivery was made today. This meat came fresh from the cart."

The twins lifted up their catch to show Mama and Papa.

"We caught these," announced Paulus. He held up a stringer with two fish on it.

Ignatius lifted a line holding a half dozen fish. "And Marco and Crispin caught all these!"

"Why do you have their fish?" Mama asked.

Marco and Crispin arrived, lugging the copper basin between them. "It was so we could carry *this*," Marco said.

Papa folded his arms. "Don't tell me you dented it *again*!"

"No," Crispin explained. "We asked Papa if we could donate it. Ignatius and Paulus said you could melt it down. Then you could use it to make a bell for the church."

Mama and Papa embraced them. They brought the boys — and the copper tub — into the villa. They invited Antonia to come, too.

"We'll be right back," Ignatius and Paulus called as they ran to the workshop.

Papa led Antonia and the neighbor boys into the room where Master Giovanni, Mistress Julia, and the pope were meeting. The boys presented the copper tub to Pope

Liberius. "It's for the church's bell," Marco explained with a bow.

The pope thanked the brothers. "I am very grateful for your gift," he told them. "And Antonia, I appreciate the meat you have brought from your father." He raised his hand in a blessing over the children.

The twins returned. Ignatius held something behind his back.

"We have a gift for you, too, Holy Father," Paulus said. Ignatius gave him a smooth, polished fishing pole. It was strung with the finest, thinnest twine Paulus ever made.

"Thank you!" the pope said.

"Now you won't just be a fisher of men," Ignatius said with a shy smile.

Paulus laughed. "You will be a fisher of *fish*, too!"

The pope practiced casting the line. "If the line were longer, I could try it out in your well," he said. "I'd like to see if I could catch anything down there." He winked at Mama and Papa.

The boys' heads snapped toward each other. They

could bring the pope all the fishing line they had and the biggest hook! They took off running.

The twins dashed into the atrium. They circled the shallow pool in the center of the room. They tore through the entry hall.

Their bare feet slapped against the stone floor as they raced from the villa. The vase on the pedestal wobbled. But this time, no one even noticed.

AUTHOR'S NOTE

This fictional story is about a real church in Rome that is dedicated to Jesus' mother, Mary. A legend says that a wealthy Roman couple, Giovanni and his wife, vowed to give their estate to the Mother of God, for they had no children to inherit their wealth. They prayed to her, asking that she show them how they could honor her.

During a night in August in the year 358, Our Lady appeared at the same time in dreams to Giovanni and his wife as well as to Pope Liberius. Mary asked that a basilica be built on a site that would be covered with snow the next day, August 5.

In the heat of that summer night, a miraculous snow fell on Esquiline Hill. The pope had the outline of the church marked in the snow. The wealthy Giovanni and his wife provided the money for the construction of the basilica. It is the first and largest Catholic church in Rome dedicated to Mary and is called Santa Maria Maggiore (Saint Mary Major). The basilica is also known as Our Lady of the Snows.

Interesting Facts About Santa Maria Maggiore

- The basilica houses a relic of the manger from Bethlehem in which Jesus was laid.
- St. Jerome, who translated the Bible into Latin around the year 400, is buried in this church.
- The ceiling of the basilica is lined with the first gold that came from the Americas, brought by Christopher Columbus to Spain's Queen Isabella and King Ferdinand. They gave the gold to Pope

Alexander VI, who was from Spain.

- St. Ignatius of Loyola celebrated his first Mass here on Christmas Day in 1538.

- It was in this church that Pope St. Pius V prayed the Rosary that won the victory of the Battle of Lepanto on October 7, 1571, when the Catholics were greatly outnumbered by Ottoman forces. Pope St. Pius V is buried here, as are several other popes.

- On March 14, 2013, the day after being elected pope, Pope Francis made a surprise visit to this church to pray and bring flowers to Our Lady.

- August 5 marks the feast day known as Our Lady of the Snows. Each year on this day during Mass at the basilica, white rose petals shower down from the ceiling as a reminder of the miraculous snowfall of August 5 in 358.

ABOUT THE AUTHOR

Claudia Cangilla McAdam is an award-winning children's author with a master's degree in theology. She loves Sacred Scripture and has always wondered what it would be like to live in the time of Jesus. Many of her books invite children to enter into those Bible stories with her. Learn more about her and request a free discussion guide for this book at ClaudiaMcAdam.com.

ABOUT THE ILLUSTRATOR

Oliver Cuthbertson has been illustrating children's books for over 15 years. His career has included working on over 100 published books with a focus on historical paintings. Born in Jordan and raised partly in Italy, Oliver moved to the United Kongdom with his family as a child. He now lives in Tunbridge Wells with his wife and two children. When not spending time with them, he enjoys board games and playing guitar.